The Case Of The

CHEERLEADING CAMP MYSTERY™

Look for more great books in

~The New Adventures of~
MARY-KATE & ASHLEY™
series:

The Case Of The Great Elephant Escape™
The Case Of The Summer Camp Caper™
The Case Of The Surfing Secret™
The Case Of The Green Ghost™
The Case Of The Big Scare Mountain Mystery™
The Case Of The Slam Dunk Mystery™
The Case Of The Rock Star's Secret™

and coming soon
The Case Of The Flying Phantom™

The Case Of The
CHEERLEADING CAMP MYSTERY™

by Lisa Fiedler

■HarperEntertainment
An Imprint of HarperCollinsPublishers

A PARACHUTE PRESS BOOK

PARACHUTE PRESS

Parachute Publishing, L.L.C.
156 Fifth Avenue
New York, NY 10010

DUALSTAR PUBLICATIONS

Dualstar Publications
c/o Thorne and Company
A Professional Law Corporation
1801 Century Park East
Los Angeles, CA 90067

♣HarperEntertainment

An Imprint of HarperCollins*Publishers*
10 East 53rd Street, New York, NY 10022–5299

ISBN 0-06-106590-0

First printing: May 2000

Printed in the United States of America

outta site!
marykateandashley.com
Register Now

Visit HarperEntertainment on the World Wide Web at
http://www.harpercollins.com

1

WE ARE THE PANTHERS!

"Cheerleading camp is the best!" I said to my twin sister, Ashley.

"I know," said Ashley. She jumped into the air and landed in a split on the grass. Her blond ponytail bounced. "Go, team!" she shouted. Then she grinned. "Sorry—I couldn't help it. Can't you just feel the team spirit around here?"

I laughed. "I feel something, all right," I said. "Hungry." I reached down to help

Ashley up. "Let's go to breakfast."

I couldn't believe Ashley and I were actually here at sleep-away cheerleading camp. We'd been looking forward to it for weeks. Especially Ashley. She's been totally into cheerleading ever since she was little.

Camp was being held at a fancy boarding school. The place was amazing. The brick buildings had ivy growing on the walls. And there was plenty of green grass, shady trees, and cool cobblestone pathways.

Ashley and I spent the day yesterday in the school's Olympic-size gymnasium, learning cheers. It was so exciting. Almost as exciting as solving mysteries for the Olsen and Olsen Mystery Agency! That's what Ashley and I do. We're detectives. We run the agency out of our attic.

But for two weeks we were going to be cheerleaders!

I glanced behind me. "Uh-oh," I said. "Look who's coming."

Ashley looked. Our roommates, Wendy Sanders and Marla Franklin, were walking up the path. It was only the start of our second day. And Wendy was already driving me a little crazy.

"If she says one more word about wanting to be captain…" I whispered to Ashley.

Ashley sighed. "Tell me about it," she whispered back.

"Hey, wait for us!" Wendy called.

Marla and Wendy ran to catch up to us.

"I forgot to tell you guys," Wendy said. "Last season I got an award for Most School Spirit." She fluffed her dark curls.

"Congratulations," Ashley said politely.

"Thanks," said Wendy. "And—oh! Did I mention that my cheerleading squad was first place in the league? I was captain. So I'm a natural choice for Panther captain here at camp."

"A natural bragger is more like it!" Marla whispered to me.

I giggled. I wasn't really angry with Wendy. Her bragging was annoying. But basically, she was okay.

"I helped to make up the winning cheer," Wendy was telling Ashley.

"Really?" Ashley said. "You know, Marla made up an amazing cheer yesterday, during the opening pep rally."

At first Wendy frowned. But then she shrugged. "That's true," she admitted. "Marla's cheer was really great."

Marla blushed. She's tall and thin, with plain, mouse-brown hair. And she's excellent at writing cheers.

"In fact," Wendy went on, "Marla is so good at making up cheers, I was thinking I'd make her chief cheer-writer when *I'm* named captain."

I just *had* to change the subject. "So is Kim coming to the meeting?" I asked Marla. Marla's older sister, Kim, is our squad's counselor-in-training. She's really nice.

Marla nodded. "This is Kim's first year as a CIT. She was a camper here for five years. She was squad captain for three."

"You know why else I should be captain?" Wendy broke in. "I'm always chosen to be on the top of the pyramid. I have very good balance."

I rolled my eyes. So much for changing the subject!

Finally, we reached the dining hall. Inside, the delicious smells of bacon and pancakes filled the air. We took our place in the food line. We saw Kim talking with some other CITs. As soon as she spotted us, she hurried over.

Marla sighed. "I bet she's going to remind me to drink all my orange juice."

"Why would she do that?" I asked. I put a grapefruit half on my tray.

"Kim always thinks she has to take care of me," said Marla.

Ashley and I exchanged glances. We

noticed that yesterday. Kim kept asking Marla if she'd remembered to stretch before doing her jumps. Then she tried to put extra sunscreen on her.

"Kim does seem to worry a little," Ashley said. She took a plate of food from the cafeteria lady. "But it would be cool to have a sister who's such a great cheerleader!"

"You *do* have a sister who's a great cheerleader," I said. I tossed my hair like Wendy. "Did I mention that my cartwheels were voted best in the universe?"

Marla and Ashley cracked up all the way to our table.

Our squad, the Panthers, sat at a table with Kim. Our table was right beside the Tigers' table. Patty O'Leary, who lives next door to Ashley and me at home, is on the Tigers' squad. We call her Princess Patty (behind her back, of course!). She's one of those kids who gets everything she wants.

Patty waved to us and we waved back.

She was wearing brand-new, expensive sneakers. On the table beside her was a fluffy pair of gold and purple pom-poms.

"I heard Patty's parents had those pom-poms made especially for her," Marla said.

"They *are* cool," Ashley said. "But I still like my lucky ones better."

"We know!" Marla, Wendy, and I said together. Then we all burst into giggles.

"You sure are crazy about those lucky pom-poms," Wendy said.

Ashley's cheeks turned red. "I can't help it," she said. "I don't let anyone touch them. Not even Mary-Kate."

"Ashley's totally superstitious about those pom-poms," I explained. "It's weird. She's usually very logical."

"Well, I'd be careful with them, too, if they were mine," Marla said. "They're so pretty, Ashley. I love the red and silver streamers."

"Yeah, but they're so old, they're falling

apart," Wendy said. "Mine are brand new."

"Hey, are you guys talking about Ashley Olsen's famous lucky pom-poms?" Patty called from the next table.

Luckily, we didn't have to answer. Coach Bradshaw, the camp director, stood up to begin the meeting. She was an athletic-looking woman with short blond hair.

"Good morning, campers," she said. "I just want to go over the schedule for the next few days. As you know, tomorrow we'll hold a competition to choose captains for each squad: the Panthers, the Tigers, the Lions, the Wildcats, the Bears, and the Dolphins. The captains will lead their squads in the All-Camp Championships. The championships will take place at the end of next week."

A murmur of excitement rippled through the cafeteria.

"You guys have a tough act to follow," Kim whispered to us. "The Panthers have won the All-Camp Championships for the last five years!"

"I've chosen three girls from each squad to compete for captain," Coach Bradshaw went on. She cleared her throat and looked down at her clipboard.

"I hope you're one of them," I whispered to Ashley. I knew how much she wanted to be a captain.

"I hope so, too!" Ashley said.

I held my breath. First, Coach Bradshaw named three campers from the Dolphins. Next she announced the captain candidates for the Lions, the Wildcats, and the Bears. Then she came to the Tigers. "Patty O'Leary!" Coach Bradshaw called.

Patty squealed so loudly that I had to cover my ears. But I uncovered them in time to hear Coach Bradshaw's next announcement.

"And trying out for Panther captain will be…"

I grabbed Ashley's hand.

"Marla Franklin!"

Marla gasped. Kim jumped up and let out a whistle that nearly shattered my juice glass.

"And Wendy Sanders!" Coach Bradshaw continued.

We all looked at Wendy. She grinned. "Of course," she said.

"And, finally," Coach Bradshaw finished, "Ashley Olsen!"

"Hooray!" I shouted. "All right, Ashley!" I gave her a big hug. Ashley looked really happy.

"Start practicing, everyone!" Coach Bradshaw told us. "And good luck to you all!"

We did an after-breakfast cheer. Then we headed out of the dining hall.

As we walked toward the dorm to get ready for practice, Patty came up to Ashley. "With me as captain, the Tigers are going to put a stop to the Panthers' winning streak!" she said. "Even your lucky pom-poms won't help!"

"Ha!" said Wendy. "Sorry, Ashley. But *I'm* going to win the competition tomorrow. With me as captain, the Panthers will whip the Tigers' tails—and everyone else's!"

Ashley, Marla, and I watched as Patty and Wendy walked off. They were arguing all the way.

Ashley turned to Marla. "Congratulations," she said.

"You, too," Marla said. She looked at the ground. "To tell you the truth, I'm kind of surprised I was picked." Then she frowned. "I wonder if Kim had anything to do with it."

"Maybe Coach Bradshaw figured that cheering talent runs in your family," I said.

Before Marla could reply, Kim ran up and threw her arms around her. "I'm so proud of you!" Kim cried. "Let's go to the staff lounge so I can braid your hair."

"But I like it the way it is," Marla protested. She was wearing a brown leather headband.

"Don't be silly," Kim said. "A nice, neat French braid is much better for a cheerleader. And I want to be sure you wear enough sunscreen. We'll be practicing out on the football field. There isn't any shade there."

Marla shook her head. "No way! I'll put on sunscreen. But not that smelly coconut kind you always wear! It makes me feel like a human macaroon cookie!"

Ashley and I couldn't help giggling.

"Fine," said Kim. She looked a little hurt. "You can wear your own sunscreen. But I really want to do your hair."

"Go ahead," Ashley told Marla. "Mary-Kate and I will meet you on the field."

"Okay," Marla said. "See you later, I guess." She followed Kim toward the athletic building, where the staff lounge was.

Ashley and I headed toward the dorm. When we got to our room, Ashley went straight to her dresser.

"That's funny," she said, frowning. "I left my lucky pom-poms right here."

"Maybe they fell behind the dresser," I said. I checked out the space between the dresser and the wall. "Nope."

Ashley got on her hands and knees. She looked under the bed.

"Maybe somebody moved them," I said.

Ashley crossed the room to the closet. She opened the closet door and looked inside. Then she checked the desk drawers. I ran over and went through Ashley's super-neat dresser drawers. Then I went through my own messy ones.

Still nothing.

Ashley sank down on her bed. "I can't believe it, Mary-Kate," she said. "My lucky pom-poms are *gone!*"

2

OUT OF LUCK

"**H**ow can I cheer without my lucky pom-poms?" Ashley wailed.

"Don't panic!" I told her. "We'll keep looking."

"But we've already searched the room," Ashley said. "Where could they be?"

I frowned. Then I glanced down at the floor. "Ashley, look!" I cried, pointing.

On the carpet were a few shreds of silver and red streamers. Ashley knelt down and picked up one of the plastic ribbons.

"These are from my pom-poms. And they lead into the hall!" she said. "Let's go!"

We tracked the trail of streamers down the hall. They led to a room that belonged to four girls from the Tigers. *Patty's* room!

The door was closed. I knocked. When no one answered, I tried the knob.

"Locked," I said. "They're probably all at the field for practice already."

Ashley studied the red and silver streamers in front of the door carefully.

"So Patty took your pom-poms," I said. "I don't get it. Why would she do that?"

Ashley sighed. "Hold on, Mary-Kate. We don't have any proof Patty took them."

I pointed at the streamers on the floor. "I call that proof!" I said. I scratched my chin thoughtfully. "Maybe Patty really does believe those pom-poms are lucky," I said. "She might think they'll help her win Tiger captain."

"Maybe," Ashley said slowly. "But still…"

I wrinkled my forehead. "I always knew Patty was spoiled," I said. "But I never thought she'd *steal* something."

"We don't know for sure she did," Ashley reminded me. "We don't even know for sure that the pom-poms were stolen."

"Well, they didn't just walk away," I said.

Ashley shrugged. "We'd better get to practice. Besides, before we accuse anyone of taking the pom-poms, we should ask if anyone's seen them."

"Okay, okay," I grumbled. Sometimes I wish Ashley wasn't so logical!

We arrived at the field just as the counselors and CITs were lining up for a demonstration cheer. Ashley and I sat down on the grass beside Marla. Wendy was there, too. Patty was sitting right behind us.

The cheer was being led by Lynn, the Tigers' CIT. Lynn was very pretty. She had a dark tan and long, curly dark hair.

"This is a special welcome cheer I wrote

for the new campers," Lynn announced. She waved to us.

Talk about team spirit. Lynn had painted her nails in black and orange stripes—Tiger colors!

I saw Kim in the lineup, too. She was smiling.

"Ready?" Lynn hollered. "Let's go!"

"Welcome campers, one and all! We're here to cheer and have a ball! Show your spirit, shout out loud! Cheerleading campers, psyched and proud!"

The cheer was great. But the best part was the ending. The counselors lifted Kim into a special throw called a basket toss. We all clapped like crazy as she went zooming up toward the sky. She came down in a graceful pike. Then she landed safely in the arms of four of her squadmates. The campers went wild.

"Wow," I said to Marla. "Kim is terrific!"

"She's a natural," Marla said proudly.

"Not like me," she added, under her breath.

"With Kim for a CIT and me for a captain," Wendy said, "the Panthers can't lose!"

I shook my head. *Did she ever give up?*

A few minutes later the counselors divided each of the five squads into minisquads of four girls each. Each minisquad had a captain candidate to lead them. Luckily, I was put in Ashley's group. A girl named Katie and another girl named Trisha were the other two members of our squad. Then Kim began handing out folders to the captain hopefuls.

"Here are some copies of cheers for you to learn," she explained. She handed Ashley the last of the three Panthers' folders. "Captains, it's your job to organize your minisquads and prepare the cheers. Later, you'll each do the cheers for Coach Bradshaw and the counselors."

I looked at Ashley. I could tell she was still upset about her missing pom-poms.

But I knew she wouldn't let that sta[n]d the way of doing her best job.

"Okay, guys. Let's start with the words," Ashley said. She quickly handed a typed sheet to each of us. "When I say 'hit it,' we'll read the words together. Okay?"

We nodded. Ashley took a deep breath.

"Ready? Hit it!"

Katie, Trisha, and I began to shout the words as we read them for the very first time.

"Two, four, six, eight, Ashley Olsen, don't you wait! If you don't want major trouble, quit the tryouts on the double!"

My jaw dropped open. I couldn't believe what we just said! And from the looks on Katie, Trisha, and Ashley's faces, neither could they.

"What kind of cheer was *that*?" asked Katie.

"That was no cheer," I said. "That was a threat!"

3

DOUBLE THREAT

Ashley looked a little pale. She nodded. "It was definitely a threat," she said.

"But why?" asked Trisha.

"That's what *I'd* like to know," I said. I took the cheers back from Katie and Trisha. All the copies were typed. And they were all photocopied onto the back of some old flyers about cheerleading camp.

Ashley peered more closely at her copy. Frowning, she held it up to her nose.

"Why don't you two go back to the dorm

and get your pom-poms?" I suggested to Katie and Trisha. "Ashley and I will use the ones the counselors are lending out."

"Okay," Katie said. "If you're sure you'll be all right, Ashley."

"I'm fine," Ashley said. "It was probably some kind of joke."

But I didn't think so. When Katie and Trisha were gone, I put my hands on my hips and frowned. "First your pom-poms disappear, now this. I think we have a mystery to solve," I said.

"So do I." Ashley pulled her detective notebook and a pencil out of her pocket. She's always prepared!

"Let's make a list of suspects. I'm putting Patty first on the list," Ashley said. "After all, we did find pieces of my pom-poms near her door."

"Okay," I said. "Patty's motive for taking the pom-poms is that she wants them for herself. But what's her motive for sending the mean cheer? Why does she want you not to try out?"

"That's a good question," said Ashley. "She's a Tiger, not a Panther. She shouldn't care whether I try out or not."

"We'll have to think about that some more," I said. "Who else is a suspect?"

"I hate to say this," Ashley said with a sigh. "But I think we need to include Marla, too. That cheer was nasty—but it was well written."

"True," I said. "And Marla does have a motive for wanting you to quit the captain's race. She's trying out against you."

"Right." Ashley added Marla to the list. "But that means Wendy has the same motive," she said. "If I dropped out, there would be less competition."

I watched as Ashley wrote Wendy's name under Marla's on the list. Then I glanced up—and saw that Wendy had left her squad. She hurried toward us, scowling.

She shoved a piece of paper at Ashley. "Did you put this nasty cheer in my folder?" she asked. She sounded hurt.

"What are you talking about?" Ashley asked. She looked at the paper. Then she looked at me. "It's the same thing!"

I showed Wendy the pages I was holding. "Ashley got a nasty cheer in her folder, too," I explained.

Wendy blinked at me. "She did?"

"Yes," said Ashley. "The cheer told me to drop out of the captain's race. Just like yours."

Wendy thought for a moment. "Then Marla must be the one who did it! She's the great cheer writer, isn't she?"

"That doesn't mean she did it," Ashley said quickly.

"But it doesn't mean she *didn't*," I said. "Marla keeps saying she isn't a very good cheerleader. Maybe she thinks that scaring you two is the only way she can possibly have a chance of winning captain."

The more I thought about it, the more it seemed as if Marla had a strong motive. Even stronger than Wendy's.

I hoped I was wrong. Marla was so nice!

"Well, there's one way to find out," Ashley said. "Let's see if Marla got a threatening cheer in *her* folder."

Ashley, Wendy, and I crossed the field to where Marla's group was practicing. We listened for a minute.

"Go Red! Go Black! Beat the Eagles! Attack! Attack!"

"Nothing threatening about that," said Ashley.

Before Ashley and I could stop her, Wendy marched toward Marla.

"Speaking of attack…" I said to Ashley.

"Uh-oh," Ashley said.

"Why did you put those nasty cheers in our folders?" Wendy yelled at Marla.

Marla looked confused. "What?"

Kim appeared behind her sister. "What's going on, Panthers?" she asked, smiling. "You're not cheering!" Then Kim noticed the looks on our faces. Her smile disappeared. "Is something wrong?"

"*Very* wrong!" I said.

Ashley took Wendy's folder from her. Then she held out the two folders containing the cheer threats to Kim. "Wendy and I got these scary messages," she said.

Kim read the cheers silently. "That's strange," she said, frowning. "It must be someone playing a mean joke."

"Well, *I* don't think it's funny," Wendy snapped. She crossed her arms. "I'm going to tell Coach Bradshaw."

"No, don't do that," Kim said quickly. "I don't think we need to bother Coach with this. It's just a bad joke. She's got copies of all the cheers in her office. I'll get rid of these phony cheers and bring back the real ones. Then you can all get on with practice."

"That's not fair," Wendy protested. "Marla's squad gets more time to practice."

But Kim was already jogging across the field.

Trisha and Katie returned with their pom-poms. Ashley told them what was happening. I went and grabbed two sets of pom-poms from a big box the counselors had brought out to the field.

Then our squad and Wendy's squad sat down in the grass and watched Marla's squad.

Marla stood in front of the others. Then she started the next cheer.

"Ready?" she shouted. Her voice came out as a squeak. She did the first arm motion—a high V. But she flung her arms up too fast and almost fell backwards.

Marla's right, I thought. *She isn't a really great cheerleader.* One of the most important things to do is to smile during a cheer. But Marla didn't smile at all. She looked like she had a bad stomachache or something.

Poor Marla! She must be really nervous.

Patty jogged by us. She was warming up by running laps around the field.

"Ha!" she laughed. "Taking breaks in the middle of practice? You Panthers will never beat us Tigers!"

"This is awful," I said to Ashley. "First we get gypped out of practice time. Then we get insulted."

"Don't worry, Mary-Kate," Ashley said.

"Why not?" I asked.

Ashley gave me a smile. "Because I know how to find out who's trying to ruin the competition!"

4

SNIFFING FOR CLUES

"**D**o you really know how we can find out who's trying to mess the contest up?" I asked Ashley.

Ashley nodded. "I'll tell you my plan later," she said. She pointed across the field. "Here comes Kim with the real cheers."

I sighed. I hate waiting around for Ashley to tell me the plan!

But I didn't have much time to think about it. Kim handed us the real cheers, and we got to work. Ashley made us repeat the cheer over and over until we knew the words by heart.

"These are the movements," she said, showing us. "Low V, clap. High V, clap. Right arm, left arm, clap, clap."

Luckily, we had lots of practice the day before, so we knew what Ashley was talking about. We practiced putting the words and the motions together. Then we worked on a simple finish.

Before we knew it, it was time for all the teams to perform their cheers.

The Panthers were the last team to perform. Marla's squad went first. They did a pretty good job. Wendy grumbled that it was only because Marla's team had more time to practice. Wendy's squad went next. They did all right. But they weren't perfect.

Finally, it was our turn.

"Celebrate! Our team is great! Elevate your mental state! Give a shout! Yell it out! Spirit's what we're all about!"

The sun glinted off the gold streamers of Ashley's borrowed pom-poms. She accidentally dropped them once, at the beginning of the cheer. But she thought fast and did a round-off to cover up her mistake.

For our ending, Trisha and I both lunged forward. Katie stood on our knees. Ashley stepped in front of us and did a split. I couldn't help grinning. This was so much fun!

Everyone clapped. "Nice job, Panthers," Coach Bradshaw said, smiling. "Good work, everyone! Now let's break for lunch."

We were supposed to have a picnic lunch outside, but it was starting to rain. So everyone headed to the dining hall.

Ashley and I walked behind the rest of the Panthers.

"So tell me!" I demanded. "How are we going to figure out who's trying to ruin the competition?"

Ashley looked around. No one was paying any attention to us. They were scrambling to get out of the rain. "Okay, listen," she said. "I noticed something weird about those fake cheers."

"What?" I asked, shaking wet hair out of my face.

"All the pages had greasy fingerprints smudged on them."

"Greasy fingerprints?" I said. "You mean, like, from eating potato chips?"

"Yes," said Ashley. "But these prints smelled like coconut!"

"Coconut, huh?" I frowned. "So we're going to have to start...*smelling* our suspects?"

"Exactly!" Ashley said. She took out her notebook. Under CLUES, she wrote GREASY SMUDGES—SMELLED LIKE COCONUT.

I sighed. "So...who do we sniff first?"

"Marla," Ashley said. "She has the strongest motive. She's good at writing cheers. And she was the only one of the three possible Panther captains who didn't get a threat."

"That's true," I said. "But I still think Wendy's a good suspect. She could have given herself a fake threat so no one would suspect her."

"And she does really want to be captain," Ashley added.

"If it *is* Wendy, though," I said slowly, "why wouldn't she give Marla a threat, too?"

Ashley sighed. "I hate to say this, but—maybe she didn't think Marla was much competition."

"She isn't," I said.

"Okay," said Ashley. "So Wendy stays on the list."

"Don't forget Patty," I said. "She could have sent the threat, too. Maybe she thinks that without a strong captain, the Panthers won't win the All-Camp Championships."

"I'll leave Patty on, then. But I think

Wendy and Marla are better suspects." Ashley put her pad back into her pocket. It was getting a little soggy from the rain.

We ran to catch up with the others. When Ashley and I entered the dining hall, we got into line right behind Wendy.

Feeling a little silly, I leaned toward her and took a sniff. But all I could smell was chicken noodle soup.

I turned to Ashley and shrugged.

"Try again," she whispered.

This time I took a huge sniff.

Wendy whirled around. "Mary-Kate, what are you *doing*?"

"Uh…I was just, um…trying to smell the tuna salad," I said quickly. "To see if there were onions in it."

Wendy looked at the divider that separated the food from the people in line. "You can smell it through the glass?"

"Mary-Kate's got a very sensitive nose," Ashley piped up.

I took another noisy sniff. "Nope. No onions. Just celery. And maybe a little black pepper...."

Wendy shook her head. Then she moved down the line.

"Well?" Ashley demanded. "Did she smell like coconut?"

"No. Wendy didn't smell like coconut at all," I told her. "But *you* have to smell Marla."

We headed for our table. Katie, Trisha, Wendy, and Marla were already there. Ashley picked an olive out of her salad. Then she plunked her tray down next to Marla's.

"That soup looks yummy," Ashley said.

"It's not bad," Marla said. She took a spoonful.

"Mind if I take a sniff?" Ashley asked.

Marla shook her head. Ashley leaned toward Marla's tray. Then she tossed the olive to the opposite end of the table.

It landed with a little splat. Marla turned to see what the sound was. Ashley swung toward Marla and took a big sniff.

I tried not to laugh.

Marla turned back to her lunch. "So—how does that soup smell?" I asked Ashley.

"Not like I expected," Ashley answered. She shook her head.

I knew what *that* meant. Marla didn't smell like coconut, either.

"Marla!" A voice came from across the dining hall.

Everyone at our table turned around. Kim had just come into the dining hall with a group of counselors. I could see Lynn's black-and-orange nails all the way across the cafeteria.

"Marla!" Kim called again. "Load up on carbohydrates! Starches, not sweets! They'll give you energy this afternoon!"

Marla's face turned bright red. She shrank down in her seat. Everyone at the

Tigers' table next to us started giggling.

"Oh, brother," said Patty. She rolled her eyes. "One Panther has lucky pom-poms. And the other has a baby-sitter! What a squad!" She gave her own pom-poms a shake. "Speaking of pom-poms," she called to Ashley, "Lynn says you'd better not drop those borrowed ones in tryouts like you did today. You'll lose major points. She says you probably dropped those pom-poms because they're heavier than your so-called lucky ones."

"She didn't drop them," Katie said hotly.

"Yeah," Tricia added. "She put them down so she could do the round-off."

I gave Ashley a thumbs-up. She must have covered really well, if Katie and Tricia believed that!

"Sure she did." Patty gave us a knowing smile. Then she left the dining hall.

"I don't need to sniff her," I whispered to Ashley. "I already know just what I'd smell. A big, hairy, stuck-up rat!"

I was hoping Ashley would laugh at that. She didn't.

"Patty's right!" she said sadly. "How can I cheer my best tomorrow with these borrowed pom-poms? They *are* heavier than mine. It throws off all my arm motions."

"Cheer up, Ashley," I said. "We'll solve the mystery before then." I secretly crossed my fingers for luck.

Ashley gave a determined nod. "You're right, Mary-Kate," she said. "Olsen and Olsen don't give up. We'll solve this case, and we'll solve it fast!"

"That's the spirit," I told her. "Now, let's go build some pyramids!"

Building pyramids is one of the most exciting parts of cheerleading. A pyramid is a like a human building. The cheerleaders stand on each other's legs, or backs, or shoulders to build a structure.

Because of the rain, the lesson was being held in the gym. The counselors spread out tumbling mats in case anyone fell.

At the beginning of the clinic, the CITs built an amazing pyramid to show us how to do it. The counselors pointed out exactly where the climbers were supposed to put their weight. They also explained how the girls on the bottom stayed steady. Then they showed us the correct way to dismount.

When the demonstration was over, Kim gave us our positions. She chose Ashley to be a climber, or "butterfly."

Kim also asked some girls to be spotters. The spotter's job is to stand in front or in back of the pyramid. She's supposed to catch the butterfly if the butterfly loses her balance. I volunteered to be a spotter.

Kim paired Ashley with Marla. Marla would be the base. Ashley would climb up on her shoulders. Kim told me to come and stand in front of them. "Spotter here," she said, pointing.

I spotted Wendy frowning at Ashley. I guess *she* wanted to be a butterfly. But Kim put Wendy behind Marla as second spotter.

Marla got into position. She lunged to the left. Ashley put her left foot on Marla's thigh. Then she grabbed Marla's hands. Next she placed her right foot on Marla's right shoulder. Then she carefully brought her left foot up and put it on Marla's left shoulder. Finally, she let go of Marla's hands, and stood up.

I bit my lip. Marla was wobbling like crazy!

"Steady!" cried Kim.

But as the warning left Kim's lips, I saw a look of panic flash across Ashley's face. Marla's shoulders slumped forward.

Ashley was going to fall!

5

A CLOSE CALL

I threw my arms up. Kim flew to my side.

Together the two of us caught Ashley before she touched the ground. Just in time!

"Phew!" I gasped.

Marla stumbled backward and bumped into Wendy. The two of them crashed to the floor.

My heart was pounding like crazy. I could see that Ashley was shaken up, too. Kim put her hands on Ashley's shoulders.

"Are you okay?" she asked.

"I'm fine," Ashley said. She swallowed hard.

Kim helped Marla and Wendy up. Then she put her arm around Marla. The two of them walked away, talking. Kim was frowning.

I stared after them. "You don't think Marla did that on purpose, do you?" I whispered to Ashley.

Ashley looked shocked. "I sure hope not."

"Well, if she *did*, it's way worse than mean cheers and stolen pom-poms!" I said. "You could have really gotten hurt!"

"I know." Ashley took a deep breath. "But it could have been an accident. It was the first time we ever tried a pyramid. It's hard." She frowned. "Could you tell what happened from where you were standing?"

"I was too busy trying to save your life!" I said.

"I guess you were. Thanks!" Ashley gave me a hug. Then she snapped her fingers. "There's something else. We have a new suspect!"

"We do?" I said. "Since when?"

"Since Kim put her hands on my shoulders," Ashley said.

"What do you mean?" I asked.

"Her hands were oily. And they smelled like coconut!" Ashley said with a big grin.

My eyes widened. "Coconut! The clue from the fake cheers!" I said. "Wow! So *Kim* is our new suspect?"

Marla came up to Ashley. She looked very upset.

"Ashley, are you all right?" she asked in a shaky voice.

Ashley nodded. "How about you?"

"I'm okay," Marla said. She bit her lip. "I am so sorry! My knees just gave way. When I felt you falling, I didn't know what to do. I'm really, really sorry."

She *sounded* sincere. And she did seem pretty shaken up. But I knew we couldn't let her off the hook. Suspects can be very sneaky sometimes. Maybe this apology was only an act. Maybe Marla really wanted Ashley to fall.

Just then Lynn ran up. "What happened?" she asked Kim.

"*I'll* tell you what happened," Wendy spoke up. "Marla and Ashley just proved something. When it comes to building pyramids, experience counts. I'm used to climbing to the top of the pyramid. *I* should be the one to do it!"

"I saw everything," Kim told Lynn. "Marla was doing her job just right. Her back was straight. Her stance was steady. I guess Ashley didn't place her foot correctly on Marla's shoulder."

I couldn't believe it. Kim was blaming the accident on Ashley! My cheeks got hot. I was about to tell Kim how unfair she was being. But Ashley touched my arm and shook her head. So I didn't say anything.

It was Katie and Trisha's turn to try the pyramid. Ashley and I flopped down on a mat.

"It wasn't your fault at all," I told Ashley.

"I know," said Ashley. "Kim was lying. That makes me more sure she should be on our suspect list."

"Kim knew it was Marla's fault," I said angrily. "But she wants her sister to be captain. So she made it sound like it was *your* fault instead." I shook my head. "That's low."

Ashley took out her notebook. She added Kim to the suspect list! "Okay. Kim's motive is that she wants me out of the competition. That way, Marla will have a better chance."

I frowned. "We'd better solve this case—fast. Otherwise, somebody may get hurt."

"Yeah," Ashley said. "Me!"

6

IN THE DARK

That night I couldn't sleep. All I could think about was the case. It was getting pretty scary. The stolen pom-poms, the threatening cheers, Ashley's close call at the pyramid class...

I sat up and tugged on Ashley's blanket.

"Are you awake?" I whispered.

"I am now!" Ashley grumbled.

I got out of bed. Then I grabbed my detective flashlight from under my pillow. We tiptoed into the dimly lit hallway.

Ashley closed the door behind her.

"I've been wondering about something," I said. "Why did Kim take those fake cheers away from us so quickly?"

Ashley thought for a moment. "That *is* suspicious," she said. "Maybe the coconut smell wasn't the only clue. Maybe we would have found another one if we'd had more time to examine the cheers."

"Let's go to the athletic building to look at them again," I said. "Kim must have left the phony cheers in the staff lounge or in Coach Bradshaw's office."

Ashley and I were almost to the stairwell when we heard a door open behind us.

"We can't let anyone see us sneaking out," I whispered. "They might report us to Coach Bradshaw!"

I quickly snapped off my light. We hurried to the stairs.

"Who is it?" Ashley asked in a low voice.

I peeked through the window in the

stairwell door. "It's Patty!" I whispered.

"Where's she going at this hour?" Ashley asked.

Patty scuffed along the hallway toward the bathroom. Then she disappeared inside. The coast was clear!

"Come on," I said. I shined my flashlight down the dark stairwell. I tried to remind myself that the creaky old dorm building was really beautiful—during the day.

We hurried down the stairs and ran outside.

The campus was empty. It was so dark and spooky!

Ashley snapped on her flashlight. The beam was weak. It was barely enough to light the cobblestone path as we headed toward the athletic building.

"It's so dark," Ashley whispered. "Are you sure we're going in the right direction?"

I was about to answer—when I felt a heavy hand come down on my shoulder!

A CHEERING DISCOVERY

"**D**on't take another step!" a deep voice boomed.

Beside me, Ashley froze. I felt as if my heart was turning handsprings inside my chest.

Slowly I turned to see who was holding my shoulder. Then I let out a sigh of relief. It was a campus security guard! He frowned at me. "What are you two campers doing outside at this hour?" he asked.

"Uh…" I began. "My sister here was…

um, sleepwalking! I had to go after her."

Ashley's mouth dropped open. She shut it fast.

"Sleepwalking?" said the security guard.

"Yes," I said. "She does that sometimes."

Ashley closed her eyes tightly and let out a loud snore.

"See?" I said. "I couldn't wake her. It's dangerous to wake up a sleepwalker."

The guard let go of my shoulder. "Well," he said, "it's also dangerous for two kids to be wandering around in the dark. Come on. I'll walk you back to your dorm."

"Yes, sir," I said.

Ashley let out another snore.

We followed the guard back to the front door of our dorm. Ashley was still pretending to be asleep. I had to open the door and guide her inside.

The guard watched as I dragged Ashley toward the stairs. Then he shook his head and walked away muttering to himself.

"He's gone," I told Ashley. She opened her eyes. We watched the beam of the guard's flashlight disappear into one of the buildings.

"Well, let's go," I said.

"Maybe the guard was right," Ashley said. She sounded worried. "Maybe we should check the staff lounge in the morning."

"But that will be too late," I said. "Tomorrow morning is the tryout for captain, remember? We have to solve the case now! Come on!"

"Okay," Ashley said. But she didn't sound too thrilled.

We left the dorm and took off again toward the athletic building. This time we made it without being spotted.

The staff lounge was in the basement, next to Coach Bradshaw's office. Luckily, one of the counselors had forgotten to close a window. Ashley and I climbed into the lounge with no problem at all.

As soon as my feet hit the floor, I smelled something strange. It wasn't a bad smell. In fact, it was sort of sweet and pleasant. And familiar. But before I could tell Ashley, I heard footsteps. They were coming from the hallway outside the lounge.

"Somebody's coming!" I whispered.

Ashley and I both dropped to our knees. Then we crawled as fast as we could into Coach Bradshaw's office. Unfortunately, that was a dead end.

Ashley gasped. "There's no way out!" she said.

"And the footsteps are getting louder!" I pointed to the desk. "Hide under there!" I commanded.

We scurried into the space beneath the large desk. The footsteps were even closer now. I held my breath.

Someone entered the office. A flashlight beam flickered around the room. I peeked out from beneath the desk—and saw a huge black shoe.

I turned back to Ashley and mouthed the word "Guard!"

Ashley and I stayed perfectly still until the guard left. Then we waited a few more minutes to be sure he was gone. Finally, we crawled out from under the desk.

"Let's check the lounge!" Ashley said.

We tiptoed out of the office. In the lounge we turned on our flashlights again. The glow filled the room with eerie shadows.

"Look at that," I said. I pointed to a basket filled with bottles of sunscreen. "I knew I smelled something sweet when we got here. It's coconut!"

"The camp must supply it for the counselors," Ashley said.

"That means Kim isn't the only one who could have left the coconut oil marks on the fake cheers," I pointed out.

"But she's still the most likely one. None

of the other counselors has a motive," Ashley said. She shined her light on a stack of clipboards beside a well-worn couch. "Mary-Kate, you check out what's clipped to those clipboards."

I lifted the top clipboard off the pile. "Schedules," I said. Then I picked up the next one. "Dorm assignments."

Ashley sighed. "Keep looking!"

"Don't rush me!" I said. I was a little nervous about being in the staff lounge at night, with all those guards snooping around. I dropped the clipboard! It slid under the couch. And it made a lot of noise.

I bent to pick up the clipboard. Then I noticed something else sticking out from under the couch. It was a piece of paper.

"Now we're getting somewhere!" I said. I read what was written on the paper. "*Two, four, six, eight, Ashley Olsen, don't you wait....*"

"Stop!" Ashley cried, covering her ears.

"I don't need to hear *that* again!"

"Sorry. You know, all of the cheers were typed," I said. "And I saw a computer and a printer in Coach Bradshaw's office."

Ashley's mouth dropped open. "You mean, Coach Bradshaw could be a suspect, too?"

"No way," I said. "She doesn't have any motive. Besides, Coach Bradshaw runs this cheerleading camp. She wouldn't want to scare her own campers, right?"

Ashley shook her head. "I guess not. Parents would never send their kids back for another year."

"I just meant that someone would need to get into Coach Bradshaw's office to use the computer," I said.

"So our suspect is probably a staff person—like Kim," Ashley said. She flopped onto the couch.

"We'd better put this clipboard back where we found it," I said. "And we should put the cheer back under the sofa, too."

"Right," Ashley said. "For all we know, Kim hid it there. If she comes back for it and finds it gone, she'll know someone's on to her."

I bent down to put the paper back, shining my flashlight under the couch. And that's when I saw them.

"Ashley!" I cried. "Look!" I reached under and pulled out what I'd found.

"My lucky pom-poms!" Ashley shouted happily. She scooped them up and hugged them.

"Kim must have taken them and hid them under here!" I said.

"That makes sense," said Ashley. "Everything is adding up!"

"So," I said, smiling. "Case closed!"

"That's right," said Ashley. She got a determined look on her face. "Now we just have to convince Coach Bradshaw!"

8

THE SUSPECT
WHO GOT AWAY

The next morning Wendy and Marla were up and out to the dining hall bright and early. They were already dressed in their Panther uniforms. Ashley and I overslept, since we'd been out so late.

"I'm glad we have the place to ourselves," Ashley said. She stepped out of the shower in her bathrobe. "It would have been weird talking to Wendy and Marla before tryouts."

"Speaking of the tryouts," I said, "we'd

better get moving or we might miss them!"

We headed back to our room from the bathroom. It was at the end of the long hallway. On our way we heard a door open. A square of light fell across the hall floor.

Hey. That light was coming from our room!

I frowned. "I thought Wendy and Marla were already gone," I said.

We squinted down the hallway. A tall figure was just stepping out of our room.

"That can't be Wendy or Marla," Ashley pointed out. "That person's way too tall."

Ashley was right. The shadowy figure leaving our dorm room was definitely taller than any camper we knew.

"Let's go after her. Hey, you!" I called. "Stop!"

We took off down the hall. The person made a mad dash for the stairwell.

Ashley was running so fast that the knot in her bathrobe belt came loose.

"Ashley look out!" I shouted. But it was too late. Her foot got tangled in the belt. She tripped and landed with a thump on her hands and knees.

I ran over. "Are you okay?" I asked.

"Yes," Ashley said, getting up. "But we'll never catch our suspect now. She's probably halfway down the stairs already."

"Let's look out the window!" I said. I barreled the rest of the way down the hall. Then I pressed my face to the window.

"Do you see anyone out there?" Ashley asked anxiously.

"I sure do," I said. "I see *everyone*."

The campus was swarming with campers. Everyone was hurrying to the football field. The captains' tryouts were going to start in ten minutes. And whoever we saw sneaking out of our room had already blended in with the crowd.

But I knew who it had to be. *Kim!*

We went back to our room. Ashley

immediately checked for her lucky pom-poms. They were still there. Phew!

Ashley quickly pulled her hair into a ponytail. I put on my uniform. Then I took Ashley's uniform off its hanger and handed it to her. While she got dressed, I went to get her lucky pom-poms.

When I picked them up, I noticed an orange streak on one of the silver streamers. It looked like a paint mark. I decided not to mention it to Ashley. There was no telling how she'd react!

I yanked the ruined silver streamer out of the pom-pom. Then I stuffed it into the pocket of my uniform skirt. With a little luck, Ashley would never know.

Ashley stepped into her cheerleading sneakers.

"Whoever that was, she wasn't here to steal my pom-poms," she said. "So what *was* she here for?"

"We can think about it on the way," I

said. "We're going to be late." I pulled Ashley out the door.

Halfway to the football field, Ashley suddenly started hopping as we walked.

"What's wrong?" I asked. "You're a Panther, not a rabbit!"

"My feet! They're so itchy!" Ashley cried. She pulled her sneakers off and started scratching her feet like crazy.

"Itchy feet?" I said. "That's weird." I picked up one of Ashley's shoes and banged it with my hand.

A small white cloud puffed out.

I picked up the other shoe and turned it over. Smelly white powder sifted out all over the place. Some of it got on my hand.

"Aha!" I shouted. I shook my hand frantically. "I know why Kim was in our room!"

"Why?" Ashley said, still scratching her feet.

I scratched my knuckles like crazy. "To put itching powder in your sneakers!"

DETECTIVE TRICK

CHEERING CODE

Hide a secret message inside a cheer! Here's how it works.

Your secret message will be the first letter of every line in the cheer. But there's one catch: the message reads backwards! The first letter of your message will begin the last line of the cheer. The second letter will begin the second-to-last line—and so on. For example, if your secret message is "Help," here's what your cheer would look like:

Please stand up
Let's shout it loud
Everyone
Help our school be proud!

No one will guess there's a secret message in your rhyme unless they know exactly what to look for!

From
The Case Of The CHEERLEADING CAMP MYSTERY™

DETECTIVE TRICK

CAN YOU HEAR A MYSTERY COMING?

Good detectives always keep their eyes open—and their ears open, too! How well can you recognize a certain sound? Try the following activity with a friend to see if your hearing is on the mark.

Put on a blindfold. Then have your friend make specific sounds and see how many of them you can figure out. The more you get right, the more it will help you to be a good detective! Here are some examples of sounds you and your friend can make to try and trick each other:

- Locking a door
- Crumpling a piece of paper
- Opening a can of soda
- Bouncing a ball
- Footsteps across a floor

Look for our next mystery...
The Case Of The *Flying PHANTOM*™

ITCHING FOR ANSWERS

Ashley looked at me in horror. "Oh, no!" she cried. "Itching powder?"

"Yes!" I began to take off my own sneakers. "Tim Park bought some once in a gag store back home. He showed it to me. I remember the smell."

"It feels like *extra-strength* itching powder!" Ashley groaned. She was really hopping up and down now, trying to scratch both feet at once. "Mary-Kate, how can I cheer like this?"

"I'm way ahead of you," I said. I handed her my shoes and socks. "Here. You can wear these. I'll wear yours."

"But they're still itchy," Ashley protested.

"It doesn't matter," I told her. I put the sneakers on. My feet immediately began to tingle, but I tried to ignore it. "Hey, I'm not the one trying out for captain," I said.

"Thanks, Mary-Kate," said Ashley, giving me a hug. "You're the best." She put on my socks and sneakers. "And Kim is definitely the worst! I can't believe she did this to me!"

The two of us hurried to the football field. But we were so late that we missed all the tryouts except the Panthers. We arrived just as Wendy was beginning her tryout cheer.

She had a huge smile on her face. "Ready?" she said to her squad. "Hit it!"

Wendy began by doing a fast windmill action with her arms. It really showed off her pom-poms.

"Panthers! Fight! Black and white. Panthers! Fight! Win tonight!" she shouted.

Wendy finished the cheer with a round-off back handspring. Then she landed in a split.

Not bad, I thought. I looked over at Ashley. I could tell that Ashley thought Wendy did a good job, too.

Everyone began to clap. Wendy had definitely impressed everyone. Then Coach Bradshaw called Ashley's name.

"I'm here!" said Ashley, catching her breath.

Coach Bradshaw nodded. "You may begin," she said.

Ashley took her place on the field. I watched from the sidelines. My feet were too itchy to climb the bleachers.

"All set? You bet! P! A! N! T! H! E! R! Panthers! The best! The best...by far!"

Ashley's cheer was upbeat and bouncy. She put a lot of energy into every move.

She lifted her knees high. And she punched her arms out straight and hard for every word. Her lucky, silver-and-red pom-poms glinted in the sunshine as she shook them.

When Ashley was done, the campers cheered just as loudly as they had for Wendy. I tried to clap for Ashley, too. It wasn't easy, though. I had to keep hopping from one foot to the other. The itching was driving me crazy!

Marla was up next. Her cheer was really clever. But she messed up four different times on the arm movements. Even though I was rooting for my sister, I did feel sorry for Marla.

But not as sorry as I felt for my itching feet!

After Marla finished, all the campers voted. We Panthers wrote our choices for captain on a slip of paper. Then we put them into the Panthers' ballot box. Coach Bradshaw told the counselors to bring all six team boxes back to the lounge. Then the counselors would vote. When they were done, Coach Bradshaw would count the votes and announce the winners for each squad.

I hopped over to Ashley. "Okay," I said. "Time's up. Let's solve this mystery right now!"

"Good idea, Mary-Kate," Ashley agreed. "You get Coach Bradshaw. I'll get Kim."

I went over to Coach Bradshaw and asked if Ashley and I could talk to her in private. She looked at me kind of funny. Probably because I was stamping my feet and hopping up and down.

A few seconds later Ashley appeared with a frowning Kim. Marla was following them. She looked confused.

"What's going on?" asked Kim.

"That's what *we'd* like to know!" Ashley said.

"Coach Bradshaw," I began. "We think

Kim has been trying to ruin the Panther tryouts for Ashley and Wendy."

Kim's mouth fell open. "What? Why would I do that?" she asked.

"Because you wanted Marla to be captain!" I said.

Coach Bradshaw's face was solemn. "This is a very serious claim, girls," she said. "Do you have any proof?"

"Yes," said Ashley. She took out her notebook. "First, my lucky pom-poms were stolen. Last night Mary-Kate and I found them hidden in the staff lounge. While we were there, we also discovered that the CITs use coconut sunscreen."

Coach Bradshaw looked puzzled. "I'm not sure I understand," she said.

Ashley went on. "At practice yesterday Wendy and I both received threatening cheers," she said. "They were typed, and they had greasy, coconut-scented fingerprints all over them. This morning someone tall enough to be a counselor snuck into our room. And she put itching powder in my sneakers."

"In *your* sneakers?" asked Coach Bradshaw. She raised her eyebrows and turned to me.

I hopped from one foot to the other. "We switched," I explained.

"So all our evidence points to a CIT," Ashley concluded.

"But why me?" Kim protested. "It could be any one of the counselors!"

"You're the only one with a motive!" I told her. "You wanted to make sure your sister Marla won the competition."

"It's true, I wanted Marla to win," Kim admitted. "But I would never cheat!"

"That's right," Marla cried. "Kim's no cheat! And besides, it doesn't matter now. I messed up my tryout so badly, I could never win."

Kim placed her hand gently on Marla's

shoulder. "That's not the point," she said. "I don't know who did all those things to Ashley and Wendy. But I do know it was a very unfair thing to do. It was wrong. Cheerleading is about spirit and team-work. Not selfish competition."

Ashley and I looked at each other. I knew she was thinking the same thing I was: Either Kim was a good faker—or she really didn't do all the things we accused her of.

Just then one of the counselors came over to tell Coach Bradshaw that they'd finished voting. It was time for her to count the votes.

Coach Bradshaw sighed. "All right, everyone," she said. "Come with me to my office. After I count the votes, we'll discuss this matter some more."

The four of us followed Coach Bradshaw in silence. I was thinking so hard about all the clues and suspects that I forgot about the terrible itching in my socks. Almost.

We crowded into Coach Bradshaw's office. Then we waited as she counted the Panthers' votes. I kept hopping up and down.

"You must be really anxious," said Kim.

"No," I told her. "Really itchy!"

Finally, Coach Bradshaw glanced up from the pile of votes. She looked very surprised. "Marla got every single vote."

"What?" Marla said. She looked at her sister in shock. "*Kim!*"

"Hey, wait a minute…" Kim began.

"That's impossible!" I said. "I voted for Ashley, not Marla."

"So did I!" Marla said.

"You did?" Kim asked, surprised.

"No way would I vote for myself," Marla said. "I never even wanted to be captain in the first place. I'd rather just stand in the background and write cheers. I was only trying out to make you happy, Kim."

Kim threw her arms around Marla. "I'm so sorry," she said. "I had no idea!"

Coach Bradshaw frowned. "Something is very wrong here."

"It sure is. Mary-Kate and Ashley were right!" Marla cried. She sounded close to tears. "This proves you did all those terrible things, Kim!"

"How does it prove anything?" Kim asked. She looked as if she might cry herself.

"You put fake votes for me in the ballot box!" Marla said. "How else could I have won?"

"No!" said Kim. "Honest, Marla, I didn't do it." She looked so hurt and upset.

All of a sudden, I stopped hopping. "Wait!" I cried. "Kim's telling the truth!"

Everyone turned to me.

"What do you mean, Mary-Kate?" asked Ashley.

"I mean," I said, "that Kim is innocent!"

10

GO, FIGHT, WIN!

"Innocent?" Ashley, Marla, and Coach Bradshaw all gasped.

"Yes," I told them. "A counselor must have switched the votes. Only the counselors were alone with the boxes after we voted. But it couldn't have been Kim! She's been with us the whole time."

"That's true," Ashley said slowly. She pulled out her notebook and studied it for a minute. "Wait, I've got it!" she said finally.

"You mean you've figured out who

changed the votes?" asked Kim, in surprise.

"No," said Ashley. "But I *do* know what the person's motive was."

"What?" I asked.

"It's the motive we thought was Patty's," Ashley explained. "Whoever did all this wanted to make sure the Panthers had a captain who wasn't a strong cheerleader. With Marla as captain, it would be easier for another squad to win the All-Camp Championships next week."

Ashley was brilliant! "That's right," I said. "So now all we have to do is figure out who switched the votes."

Ashley and I looked at each other.

"We're going to need your help, Coach," I said. Here's my plan…."

After I explained my plan, we all headed out of the office. By now the rest of the campers had gathered outside the athletic building. They were curious about what was going on. And they were getting impatient.

"Who won captain?" Wendy called.

"That's what we need to find out. We have a little problem," Coach Bradshaw said. "Counselors, I need you to step into the lounge, please!"

A low murmur of confusion ran through the campers.

All the counselors and CITs stepped into the staff lounge. Coach Bradshaw asked them to stand in a line. "Mary-Kate and Ashley have some questions for you," she said. "Please answer them." She glanced at Ashley and me. "Go ahead, girls."

"Do you all use the sunscreen from the lounge?" Ashley asked the counselors.

The Dolphins' counselor, a dark-haired girl named Nancy, raised her hand. "I don't," she said. "I'm allergic to it."

I stepped forward. "Do you mind if I sniff you?"

Nancy looked puzzled, but she held out

her arm for me to sniff. Her sunscreen smelled like pineapple.

"Okay," I said, nodding. "Please step out of the line."

Ashley was staring at the remaining CITs. "Remember the girl we saw sneaking out of our room?" she whispered to me.

"Yes," I said. "She was tall."

Ashley nodded. Then she pointed to Alicia, the Bears' petite, red-haired CIT. She wasn't much taller than we were. "You can step out, too," Ashley told her.

Now we had only three suspects left.

Ashley turned back to them. "Was anyone alone with the ballot boxes?" she asked.

All three of the suspects raised their hands.

"We voted one at a time," said Lynn, with a shrug. "We were all alone with the boxes."

I gasped as Lynn lowered her hand. She was still wearing her tiger-striped nail polish. And that's when I made the connection. I pointed to Lynn.

"Maybe so!" I cried. "But *you* were the one who switched the Panthers' votes!"

The Tigers' CIT turned pale. "*Me?*"

"Yes!" I said, walking over to her. "And you also wrote those threatening cheers. They were mean, but they were good! And we know you're good at writing cheers. You wrote that welcome cheer the counselors did yesterday."

Lynn gulped. Everyone was staring at her now.

"And," I continued excitedly, "*you* stole Ashley's pom-poms!"

"You can't prove that!" Lynn gasped.

"Yes, I can," I told her. "You told Patty that the pom-poms Ashley borrowed yesterday were heavier than her lucky ones. That means you must have actually held the pom-poms. And that's impossible— unless you took them. Because Ashley never lets anyone touch them."

"I could have just guessed they were lighter," Lynn said.

"Maybe," I replied. "But there's even more evidence that points to you."

I pulled the crumpled, orange-streaked streamer out of my skirt pocket. Then I held it beside Lynn's nails. Her orange stripes were the exact same color as the smear on the streamer.

"The orange is a perfect match!" I said. "You must have stolen the pom-poms while your polish was still wet. That's how it got on this streamer."

"My poor lucky pom-poms!" Ashley cried. She turned to me. "Hey, how come *I* didn't know about that clue?"

"Sorry," I said. "Um, let's talk about that later."

Coach Bradshaw looked at Lynn. "Is all of this true?" she asked.

Lynn looked at the floor. "Yes," she confessed. "I'm sorry, Coach. I did do all those things. But only because I was tired of seeing the Panthers win every year. It didn't seem fair."

"What *you* did wasn't fair, either," Kim said.

"I know that now," said Lynn. "And I'm really, really sorry. At the time, I thought I was helping my squad. You know, being loyal. Now I realize I was just being a cheat." She turned to Ashley and Marla. "I'm sorry, guys."

"It's okay," said Marla.

"It's all right," said Ashley.

Coach Bradshaw looked stern. "Lynn, you and I need to have a talk."

Just then there was a knock on the office door. "Hey! I want to know who the Panther captain is!" Wendy shouted.

Coach Bradshaw sighed. "I guess everyone will have to vote again," she said.

"No they won't," Lynn said. She stepped

over to the couch and picked up a back-pack that was lying next to it.

"This is where I hid the real votes," Lynn explained. She unzipped the pack and pulled out a neat stack of ballots.

"I'll count them," Kim offered.

We all watched eagerly as Kim read the slips of paper.

Coach Bradshaw marked down the results on her clipboard. "It's a tie between Ashley and Wendy," she announced finally. She smiled. "Looks like we've got co-captains!" she said.

"Cool!" said Ashley.

Coach finished counting the votes for all the other squads. Then we all went outside, and she announced the winners. Patty was the Tigers' captain. She beamed happily.

When Wendy heard that Ashley was going to be cocaptain, she looked disap-pointed for a second. But then she grinned. "Hey, with the two of us leading the

Panthers," she said, "we're sure to win the All-Camp Championships!"

"We'll see about that!" Patty said, sniffing.

I threw my hands up. "I can't take this anymore!" I shouted.

"Can't take what?" asked Ashley. "All this arguing about who's going to win the All-Camp Championships?"

"No," I said. I dropped to the grass and tugged off Ashley's sneakers. "I can't take this *itching*!"

Everyone laughed.

"You can wear my sneakers, Mary-Kate," Marla offered. "I've made a big decision. I'm going to finish camp as a cheer writer, not a cheerleader."

"That's a wonderful idea, Marla," said Coach Bradshaw.

"I think so, too," Kim said.

"In fact," Marla added, "I've just come up with a new cheer. Especially for Mary-Kate and Ashley."

"Let's hear it!" I said.

Marla stood up straight. She shouted in a clear voice:

"Everywhere we go, people wanna know, who we are, so we tell them, we are the Olsens, the mystery-solving Olsens!"

When Marla finished, we all clapped and whistled. Then everyone hurried out to the field again. It was time for our first official practice with our new team captains. And after that there was an all-camp swim at the pool. I couldn't wait!

"Hey, Ashley," I said, as we took up our positions on the field. "Can I borrow your lucky pom-poms?"

"No way!" Ashley said. She clutched her precious pom-poms a little tighter.

"Just kidding," I said, with a grin. I didn't need them, anyway.

Now that we'd cracked this case, Ashley and I had plenty to cheer about!

Hi from both of us,

Ashley and I were off for a week at the Air and Space Museum in Washington, D.C. But when we got there, a guard told us one of the planes was haunted!

No way, we thought. *There's no such thing as ghosts.* But how else could we explain the glowing red handprint that appeared on the plane's wings—right in front of our eyes? Or the eerie moans that came from inside the cockpit? Yikes! Maybe we couldn't!

Are you brave enough to find out more? Check out the next page for a sneak peek at *The New Adventures of Mary-Kate & Ashley: The Case of the Flying Phantom.*

See you next time!

Mary-Kate Olsen   *Ashley Olsen*

A sneak peek at our next mystery…

The Case Of The
Flying PHANTOM™

"Come join the group," the museum guide called to me and Ashley.

Ashley and I hurried over. If we were ever going to find out the truth about the haunted plane, we'd need all the facts. And this was the perfect place to start.

"As I was saying, I'm Skip Henderson," the museum guide said. "If there's anything you want to know about the *Flying Phantom*, I'm the guy to ask."

"It looks like a regular old plane to me," I whispered to Ashley.

Skip went on, "The way this baby could fly was unbelievable. The Duncan Brothers' design made the *Phantom* easier to control than any other plane of its time."

I stared up at the plane. It *was* pretty cool. I tried to imagine that it was the middle of World War I. The *Phantom* was flying above us with its guns blasting....

Suddenly, Ashley squeezed my arm—hard. "Mary-Kate, look!" she said.

"Amazing, isn't it?" I murmured.

"Don't you see?" Ashley asked.

"What are you talking about?" I said. Then I *did* see.

The Phantom was shaking!

"Everybody stay calm!" Skip called out. But he didn't sound calm at all.

The Phantom shook harder. Then it started to rock back and forth on its metal cables—all by itself!

And then the Phantom started to moan. You could hear the terrible sounds all over the room. And they were getting louder.

Planes don't moan, I told myself bravely. But ghosts do!

Do you have
all the Mary-Kate
and Ashley books?

Turn the page
to find out!

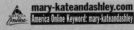